THE DOLLS' HOUSE FAIRY

For Clara

ORCHARD BOOKS

338 Euston Road, London NW1 3BH

Orchard Books Australia

Level 17/207 Kent Street, Sydney, NSW 2000

First published in 2009 by Orchard Books

First published in paperback in 2010

ISBN 978 1 84616 909 0

Text and illustrations © Jane Ray 2009

The right of Jane Ray to be identified as
the author and illustrator of this work
has been asserted by her in accordance
with the Copyright, Designs and
Patents Act, 1988.

A CIP catalogue record for this book
is available from the British Library.

10 9 8 7 6 5 4 3 2 1

Printed in China

Orchard Books is a division of
Hachette Children's Books,
an Hachette UK company.
www.hachette.co.uk

THE DOLLS' HOUSE FAIRY

Jane Ray

ORCHARD BOOKS

ROSY LOVED HER DOLLS' HOUSE.

It was her favourite thing in the whole world because her dad had built it just for her. Rosy and Dad made the furniture together and collected all sorts of things to put in the different rooms. She played for hours, making up games and stories for the dolls that lived there.

The little house was perfect.

On Saturday mornings, Dad and
Rosy always got up early.

"Just me and my Rosy Posy,"
Dad sang, as he made hot chocolate
and eggy bread for breakfast.

Then Rosy and Dad had fun together, making extra things for the dolls' house. It was Rosy's favourite time.

But one wild and windy Saturday, when Rosy woke up, everything was different . . .

Granny was in the kitchen. She gave Rosy a big hug and told her that Dad had become ill in the night. Mum had taken him to hospital. Granny told Rosy not to worry – Dad would be home as soon as he was better.

But Rosy did worry. The wind whistled around the
garden and rattled at the windows and, for the first time ever
on a Saturday, Rosy's Dad wasn't there.

Rosy went to play with her dolls' house – she thought it might make her feel better.

But when she opened the front, she gasped with surprise!
Something was different . . .

It looked as if
a whirlwind had
blown through
the house!
Everything
was topsy-turvy
– even the dolls
looked surprised.

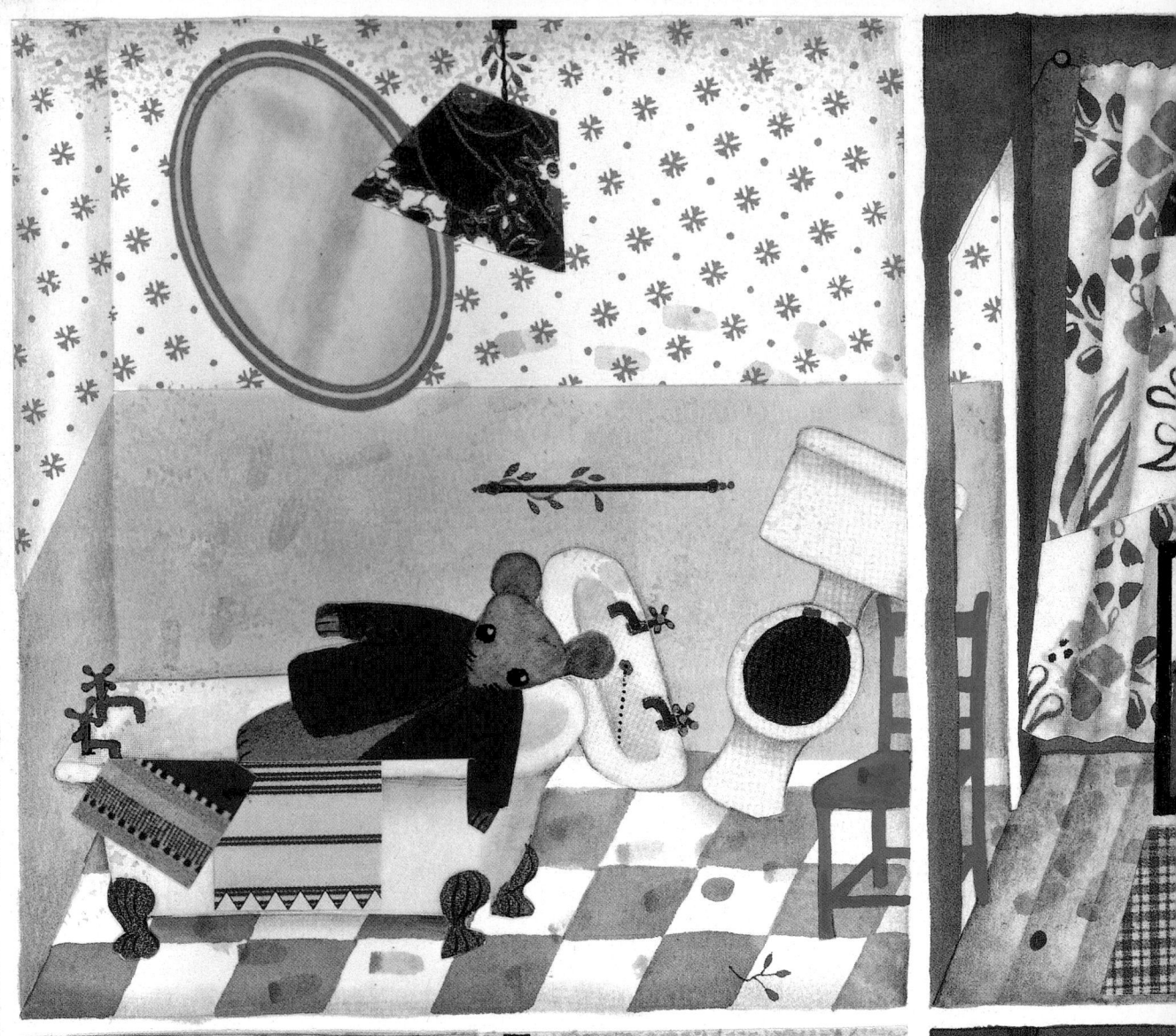

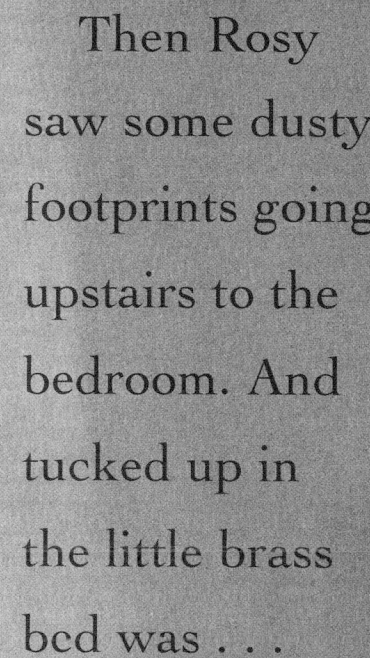

Then Rosy
saw some dusty
footprints going
upstairs to the
bedroom. And
tucked up in
the little brass
bed was . . .

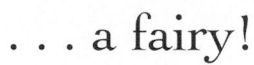 

. . . a fairy!

The fairy sat up, rubbing her eyes and yawning.

"Hello," she said. "I'm Thistle. I'm going to stay for a few nights, because I've hurt my wing. It's much nicer here than sleeping in a flower in the garden. You don't mind, do you?"

Rosy was enchanted. She didn't mind at all. It was so exciting to have a real fairy in her dolls' house! Besides, she felt sorry for the fairy with her hurt wing.

Thistle's hair stuck up all around her head like a dandelion clock. She was dressed in leaves and petals and she had very muddy feet.

"I'm ever so hungry," Thistle said, "but the food in the kitchen is just pretend. What's for breakfast?"

Rosy ran down into the windy garden and picked
raspberries and rose petals and all sorts of things to make
a perfect fairy breakfast.

She filled a dolls' house cup with rainwater and took it back to Thistle. But it wasn't Thistle's idea of a perfect breakfast.

"Have you got any crisps?" she asked.

Rosy couldn't help noticing that Thistle was very messy. She ate her crisps with her mouth open and spilled her drink all down her front. But Rosy didn't mind. She just wanted to take care of the little fairy.

Rosy didn't tell anyone about Thistle. She kept her bedroom
door closed and Rosy and Thistle played together in secret.
The fairy had made herself quite at home in Rosy's dolls' house.

At bathtime, Thistle splashed about in the dolls' house bath like a sparrow in a puddle. Then Rosy rubbed some cream on Thistle's sore wing and put a tiny piece of sticking plaster on it to make it better.

That evening, Mum came
home from the hospital. She told
Rosy that Dad was feeling much
better and would soon be home.

And when Rosy settled down
to sleep, she could see a tiny
fairy light glowing in the dolls'
house and she didn't feel quite so
worried about Dad any more.

As the days passed, Thistle began to feel better too. And as the fairy's wing got stronger, Rosy helped her to practise flying again.

Thistle wasn't like all the sweet little fairies in Rosy's storybooks. She was funny and noisy and full of mischief. She bounced on the bed and drew on the walls. She tried on all the dolls' clothes and moved the furniture into funny places. She spilt things and she dropped things and she scattered fairy dust everywhere.

But Rosy loved her.

Then, at last, one sunny afternoon, the front door opened and Dad was home! Rosy flung her arms around him. She was so happy he was back!

They all sat down together and ate the special cake that Rosy and Granny had made.

After tea, Rosy cuddled up to Dad.

"Just me and my Rosy Posy," he smiled. "Have you been busy with the dolls' house while I've been away?"

Rosy whispered in his ear and told him all about Thistle and how she had been helping to make her better. She also told him about how messy and mischievous Thistle was.

Dad listened very carefully.

"Do you think I could meet her too?" he asked.

Together, they went up to Rosy's room and opened the front of the dolls' house.

There was mess everywhere, but Thistle was nowhere to be seen.

"She was here. She was!" cried Rosy.

Dad gave her a big cuddle.

"I can see she was!" he laughed. "You must have done such a good job of looking after Thistle that now her wing is better and she has flown away home."

Together, Rosy and Dad picked up all the furniture, tidied the pretend food and carefully put the tiny cups and plates back on the table. They cleaned the scribbles off the walls and blew away the last of the fairy dust.

But Dad left out a tiny piece of cake for Thistle,
just in case . . .